For Jasmine

Text copyright © 1993 by Vivian French
Illustrations copyright © 1993 by John Prater

First U.S. edition 1993
Published in Great Britain in 1993
by Walker Books Ltd., London.

Library of Congress Cataloging-in-Publication Data:

Prater, John.
Once upon a time / conceived and illustrated by John Prater ;
text by Vivian French.
Summary: A bored boy's world is suddenly populated by three
house-building pigs, a girl wearing a red hood, and other familiar
nursery characters.
[1. Characters and characteristics in literature—Fiction.
2. Stories in rhyme.] I. French, Vivian. II. Title.
PZ8.3.P85On 1993   811'.54—dc20 [E]   92-53139
ISBN 1-56402-177-7

10 9 8 7 6 5 4 3 2 1

Printed in Hong Kong

The artwork for this book was
done in watercolor and crayon.

Candlewick Press
2067 Massachusetts Avenue
Cambridge, Massachusetts 02140

Once UPON A TIME

Conceived and illustrated by John Prater
Text by Vivian French

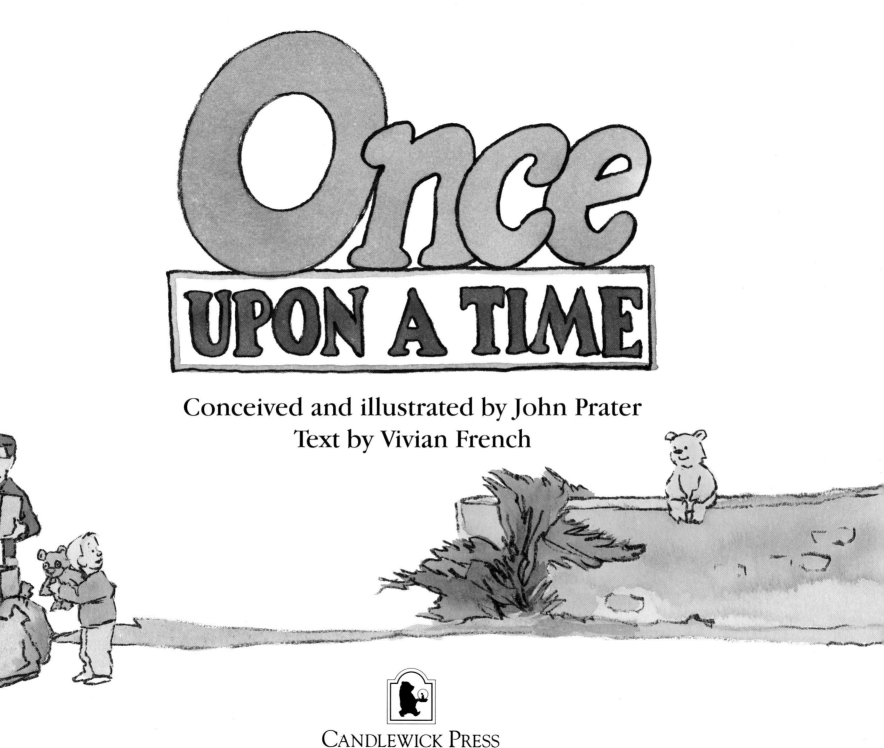

CANDLEWICK PRESS
CAMBRIDGE, MASSACHUSETTS

Early in the morning,
Cat and me.
Not much to do.
Not much to see.

Dad's off to work now,
Mom's up too.
Not much to see.
Not much to do.

Day's getting older,
Sun's up high.
Wave to a little girl
Hurrying by.

Mom's cleaning windows.
There's a bear.
He's making a fuss
About a chair.

Ride my tricycle
For a while.
There's an egg
With a happy smile.

Mom's in the garden,
Laundry's dry.
Why do babies
Always cry?

We've got sandwiches—
Cheese today.
Why's that wolf saying,
"Come this way"?

I like jumping
To and fro.
That wolf's howling.
He's hurt his toe.

Mom's drinking coffee
By the door.
I can jump
That far and more!

Sun's going down now
In the sky.
Here's Dad home again!
We say, "Hi!"

Dad's washing dishes.
I look out.
Did I hear someone
Prowling about?

Time for my story.
I yawn and say,
"Nothing much happened
Around here today."